little Miss Stubborn

by Roger Hargreaves

WORLD INTERNATIONAL

Little Miss Stubborn was, as you might imagine, extraordinarily stubborn.

Once she had made her mind up there was no unmaking it.

If she decided to go out, she went out.

Even when it was pouring with rain!

One Sunday, when it wasn't raining,
she decided to take the bus
to Mr Strong's house.

Why?

Because she had run out of eggs.

And, as everybody knows,
Mr Strong always has lots of eggs.

As the bus arrived, Mr Nosey walked by.

Being nosey, he couldn't help asking:

"Where are you going, Little Miss Stubborn?"

"To Mr Strong's house," she said.

"But this bus doesn't go anywhere near there!"

But Little Miss Stubborn took the bus anyway.

And you won't be surprised to hear it didn't go anywhere near Mr Strong's house.

It went to Coldland.

A country where it is so cold
that everybody has a cold all year round.

"What a charming place!" she said, shivering
and trying to look as if she had really planned
on coming to Coldland in the first place.

Which of course she hadn't.

As you know.

She ran along a path to keep warm.

"ATISHOO!" somebody sneezed all of a sudden.

It was Mr Sneeze.

"If I were you," he warned, "I wouldn't
take … ATISHOO! that path. It's icy! ATISHOO!"

"I'll take it if I want to!" snorted
Little Miss Stubborn.

And she followed the path.

But can you guess what happened?

WHOOOOOOSH!

She slipped on the ice!

"That was fun!" said Little Miss Stubborn.

But of course it wasn't.

She came to a fork in the path.

"I shall go this way," she said,
taking the right hand path.

"You're making a big mistake!" said a worm,
popping his head through the snow.
"This way isn't safe."

"Don't be silly!" cried Little Miss Stubborn
and started off down the path.

She should have listened to the worm!

Before she had gone very far
an avalanche of snowballs fell on top of her!

One of the snowballs rolled off the path
and rolled and rolled down a very steep hill.

And, inside it,
Little Miss Stubborn rolled and rolled
down the very steep hill as well.

The snowball rolled a very long way,
all the way into a different country
where it melted.

As luck would have it,
Little Miss Stubborn found herself
outside Mr Strong's front door.

She was soaked to the skin.

"My goodness! You're wet through!"
said Mr Strong.
"Quick, come in and dry yourself
before you catch a cold."

"I don't catch colds," said Little Miss Stubborn.
"Anyway, I've come for some eggs.
Out of my way!"

"That's no way to behave," said Mr Strong.

"Rubbish!" snorted Little Miss Stubborn.

Still wet through,
she marched into Mr Strong's kitchen.

Without a please or a thank you,
she helped herself to a large bowl of eggs.

"You could at least ask," said Mr Strong.

"ATISHOO!" sneezed Little Miss Stubborn.

"I told you you'd catch a cold," said Mr Strong.

"I don't catch colds," said Little Miss Stubborn,
and sneezed again, "ATISHOO!"

She was so hungry by this time
that, there and then, she made herself
an enormous omelette.

It was gigantic.

It was so big that it won't even fit on the page!

Then she began to eat her enormous,
gigantic omelette.

And the more she ate, the more worried
Mr Strong became:
"You'll make yourself ill," he said.

"Fiddlesticks," snorted Little Miss Stubborn,
and because she was who she was,
she finished that enormous, gigantic omelette.

And there is not much more to add.

Other than now you know how
extraordinarily stubborn
Little Miss Stubborn is!

Stubborn to the very end ...
the very end of this story.

SPECIAL OFFERS FOR MR MEN AND LITTLE MISS READERS

In every Mr Men and Little Miss book you will find a special token. Collect only six tokens and we will send you a super poster of your choice featuring all your favourite Mr Men or Little Miss friends.

And for the first 4,000 readers we hear from, we will send you a Mr Men activity pad* and a bookmark* as well – absolutely free!

Return this page with six tokens from Mr Men and/or Little Miss books to:
Marketing Department, World International Limited, Deanway Technology Centre, Wilmslow Road, Handforth, Cheshire SK9 3FB.

Your name:_____

Address:_____

_____

_____ Postcode: _____

Signature of parent or guardian: _____

I enclose **six** tokens – please send me a Mr Men poster ☐

I enclose **six** tokens – please send me a Little Miss poster ☐

We may occasionally wish to advise you of other children's books that we publish. If you would rather we didn't, please tick this box ☐

*while stocks last   (Please note: this offer is limited to a maximum of two posters per household.)

Collect six of these tokens. You will find one inside every Mr Men and Little Miss book which has this special offer.

1 TOKEN

Join the
MR.MEN & *Little Miss*
Club

Treat your child to membership of the long-awaited Mr Men & Little Miss Club and see their delight when they receive a personal letter from Mr Happy and Little Miss Giggles, a club badge **with their name on**, and a superb Welcome Pack. And imagine how thrilled they'll be to receive a card from the Mr Men and Little Misses on their birthday and at Christmas!

Take a look at all of the great things in the Welcome Pack, every one of them of superb quality (*see box right*). If it were on sale in the shops, the Pack alone would cost around £12.00. But a year's membership, including all of the other Club benefits, costs just **£7.99** (plus 70p postage) with a 14 day money-back guarantee if you're not delighted.

To enrol your child please send **your** name, address and telephone number together with **your child's** full name, date of birth and address (including postcode) and a cheque or postal order for £8.69 (payable to Mr Men & Little Miss Club) to: Mr Happy, Happyland (Dept. WI), PO Box 142, Horsham RH13 5FJ. Or call 01403 242727 to pay by credit card.

Please note: We reserve the right to change the terms of this offer (including the contents of the Welcome Pack) at any time but we offer a 14 day no-quibble money-back guarantee. We do not sell directly to children - all communications (except the Welcome Pack) will be via parents/guardians. After 31/12/96 please call to check that the price is still valid. Please allow 28 days for delivery. Promoter: Robell Media Promotions Limited, registered in England number 2852153.

The Welcome Pack:

✓ Membership card
✓ Personalized badge
✓ Club members' cassette with Mr Men stories and songs
✓ Copy of Mr Men magazine
✓ Mr Men sticker book
✓ Tiny Mr Men flock figure
✓ Personal Mr Men notebook
✓ Mr Men bendy pen
✓ Mr Men eraser
✓ Mr Men book mark
✓ Mr Men key ring

Plus:

✓ Birthday card
✓ Christmas card
✓ Exclusive offers
✓ Easy way to order Mr Men & Little Miss merchandise

All for just £7·99! (plus 70p postage)